"Get serious, you guys," Aimee said. "It's just a local show."

"That's right. It's a local show that everyone in Atlanta watches. It's a little TV appearance that is probably going to change our whole lives," I replied. I was really getting nervous.

Even Linda Jean and Joy, the other members of the Forever Friends Club, were worried. We were especially nervous when we found out that the TV crew was going to film us at one of our parties.

But as we began the party, our worries seemed unnecessary. Everything was running smoothly. I was enjoying myself so much that I almost forgot about the cameras—until the dog...

Friends To The Rescue!

Cindy Savage

Cover illustration by Richard Kriegler

To the Grembers of the Moop
My Forever Friends

Published by Willowisp Press, Inc.
401 E. Wilson Bridge Road, Worthington , Ohio 43085

Copyright ©1989 by Willowisp Press, Inc.

Printed in the United States of America
10 9 8 7 6 5 4 3 2 1

ISBN 0-87406-380-9

One

I'VE been a member of the Forever Friends Club for—well—forever. But being a member has never been as fun as it has been this summer.

Until two years ago, we had been baby-sat by Abby Marshall, my friend Joy's mom. Then she stopped just watching us, and she started to keep us busy by paying us to do odd jobs for her like washing the car and mowing the lawn. And this summer we started our own business called Party Time!

Party Time started when Linda Jean Jacobs, the newest member of our club, came up with the idea that we could actually put on parties for younger kids and make money doing it. Since then we have done 10 parties. But now something even more exciting is going to happen. We're all going to be on television! I can't believe that I, Kristina Branch, will be on television.

"Isn't it great?" Aimee asked. "When I told my dad about our business, I didn't really expect him to ask us to be on his TV show."

"I'm not surprised," said Joy, pushing her long, blond hair out of her face so that she could attack her sundae. "Mr. Lawrence knows a good news story when he hears one." She smoothed her hair a little and struck a movie star pose with her dark glasses on the end of her nose.

Linda Jean teased. "We're not famous enough to be newsworthy. If Aimee's dad wasn't a popular talk show host, we wouldn't stand a chance," she added reasonably.

We were all sitting at Juliet's Family Creamery eating ice cream. It's an open, airy place with lots of plants and tables that have outdoor umbrellas.

It was the perfect place to talk over the disaster of a party that we had just finished doing for Linda Jean's stepbrother, Josh. I say disaster because everything that *could* go wrong at a party *did* go wrong! The cake was a flop. The kids wouldn't pay attention. There was a lot of screaming, and one four-year-old boy bit another boy. As we left the party, all the kids told us that they had a good time. I'm not sure that they were telling the truth, but at least they were polite.

"What happens if the camera crew comes to one of our parties, and it turns out like the one we just gave for Josh?" Linda Jean asked.

"Yeah," I added, "soggy cakes and kids running wild are not going to make a very good impression. No one would want to hire us if they saw that."

Abby had been sitting quietly at our table listening to us talk. She's the main reason why we even started Party Time. When Abby decided to go back to work after years of staying home with us, she hired us to help prepare food for her catering business. It was at her first event, a garden club party where the kids were running wild, that we had the idea to start Party Time.

"I think you girls need to remember that most of your parties have turned out great. Glen's party went well. The kids loved the dinosaur theme, and little Amanda Klein's rainbow birthday was a big hit."

Linda Jean sighed and looked across the street at the kids playing on the playground.

After a few minutes, she said, "I'm sorry. I'm sure the party would have gone well if I hadn't been so determined to hate my new step-brother. My mom and I had a long talk upstairs while all of you were serving refreshments downstairs. Thanks for covering for me, you guys."

Linda Jean looked as if she was about to cry. I put my hand on her shoulder. She glanced from me to the group, and then she smiled.

"I'm sure that things will get better now between my mom and me. We are going to spend more time together, just the two of us. And Josh and Stephanie really are cute kids. I guess I need to give them a chance like everyone has been telling me to do," Linda Jean said.

We all smiled at Linda Jean's comment. One of the nicest things about the Forever Friends Club is that we all talk to each other about everything, and we really try to help each other with our problems. Linda Jean joined our club two years ago, when she moved to Atlanta after her parents got divorced. Linda Jean had been living with her father, and things had been going great until her mother moved to town with a new husband and family. It was really tough for Linda Jean to get used to a new stepdad, stepsister, and stepbrother all at once. But the Forever Friends Club helped her work it out by being there for her when she needed us.

The rest of us—Joy Marshall, Aimee Lawrence, and me, Kristina Branch—started the club many years ago. The three of us have lived on Honeybee Court all of our lives, and we got together as babies when Abby, Joy's mom, started baby-sitting us. It seems like we've known each other forever, and we've always shared our secrets, dreams, and special moments.

And this summer we were sharing our own business! Abby's Catering and Party Time were more successful than we had ever imagined they would be. It's been the best summer ever!

"Let's get back to the TV show," Aimee said. "Which party should we ask them to film?"

"More importantly, what should we wear?" I asked.

"Well, we know what you're going to wear, Krissy," Joy replied. "You'll wear your clown suit."

9

"And you'll be wearing one of your dance outfits that goes along with the theme of the party," Linda Jean said. "It's Aimee and I who don't have regular costumes."

"I've heard that bright colors are best," Abby mentioned as she scooped up the last of her sundae.

It may seem strange that we were devouring ice cream right after we had been at a birthday party, but it was a Party Time rule that the workers can't eat on the job.

"I've heard that you have to put on a lot of makeup just to have it show up under the lights," Joy said.

Joy knew more about performing than the rest of us. I asked, "Is that true? I don't even have any makeup."

"I only know about dance recitals," Joy said. "We use a lot of makeup because we're far away from the audience. The lights are really hot, so we have to powder our faces all the time to prevent shining because we're sweating."

"I don't think you have to make yourself up like a clown—pardon me, Krissy—for your face to show up on TV," said Aimee. "How you act is more important than what you look like."

"What do you mean?" Linda Jean asked.

"The most important thing," Aimee continued, "is to act natural. My dad always tells his guests just to be themselves."

"That will be easy for you!" I exclaimed. "You've been around cameras and television studios all your life. If someone shoves a microphone in your face, you can always come up with something to say. Sometimes I think you invented the word *ham*."

Everybody laughed, including Aimee. "You've got to be a little crazy to hold the kids' attention," she protested.

"You do a good job of that!" Linda Jean shouted over the laughter.

"Do you mean that I'm good at being crazy or at singing songs to the kids?" Aimee asked as she giggled.

"Both!" we all yelled at once.

We put our server's tip on the table and got up to leave. "Let's face it," I said. "We all had to be a little crazy to start a business and expect to get paid, when none of us had any experience in any kind of business. Most 13 year olds can't say they've done that."

"Let's hear it for being crazy!" Aimee shouted.

We cheered loudly, and every customer in

the place looked at our table to see what the commotion was all about.

"We could do one of two things," I whispered. "We could hang our heads and tiptoe out the door—"

"Or?" everyone asked at the same time.

"Or, now that we have everyone's attention, we could pass out fliers to attract more business," I said, thinking practically.

Naturally, we passed out fliers.

Two

MONDAY morning we had our first meeting with Mr. Lawrence to discuss the television show that was going to feature the Forever Friends Club. We met at Aimee's house before Mr. Lawrence had to leave for work. His job at WBCC is complicated. He hosts the evening news four times a week, and on weekends he has two special shows. One of those shows is called *Moving On*, and it's about famous black people in current or past history like Martin Luther King, Jr., Harriet Tubman, black astronauts, and black presidential candidates. The other weekend show that Mr. Lawrence does is called *Weekend Mag*, and it's about local happenings and local people. The Forever Friends Club is going to be on *Weekend Mag*.

"I think a segment on Party Time will be a hit because viewers just love to see success stories, particularly if enterprising young people are involved," Mr. Lawrence said.

"Party Time is unique to Atlanta," remarked Ms. Moore, the show's producer. "The fact that each of you brings a special talent to the business is great." She looked at her notes. "Aimee is the craft and song expert. Krissy is the clown and magic expert. Linda Jean is the animal fanatic, and Joy is the dancer." She stuck her pencil behind her ear and looked us over. "It's fabulous! The viewers will love it!"

We smiled and looked at each other shyly. Ms. Moore seemed to be in constant motion as she sat, stood, paced, and took notes. Aimee's dad said that she was one of the best producers around. I wondered if Kitty has met her.

Kitty is my younger sister. She's only nine years old, but she is already a famous model. She poses for magazine ads and does television commercials. Her success has sort of gone to her head. We seem to get along okay if I avoid her and her career as much as possible.

Still, I was curious about Kitty's popularity, and I asked Ms. Moore if she knew her.

"Oh, sure. Everyone knows Kitty Branch," she replied.

It figures, I thought. *No matter what I do, Kitty beats me to it. She might as well be my older sister.*

Mr. Lawrence was talking. "So, what we'll need from you girls is a schedule of the parties that you will be putting on during the next two weeks and your ideas about which ones may be the best to film. Think big," he advised. "A camera crew takes up a lot of space in someone's home."

"Of course, we'll have to ask for permission from the people whose child we're doing the party for," Joy said. "Some people may not want their child's party on TV."

"You're absolutely right, Joy," Mr. Lawrence said. "I'll give you until Wednesday to choose and to call your clients. Call me at my office to let me know which party you've selected to be filmed."

The meeting was over, and I hadn't felt nervous once. But Mr. Lawrence has a way of making people feel at ease, both on and off the air. His smile is contagious. People trust him to make them look good.

Aimee Lawrence had her father's smile and his energy. She could keep a group busy for hours by having them sing songs. Still, I wondered how she would act on camera. *Would she be nervous? I knew I would be!*

I wanted to ask the others if they felt the same jitters that I did from just thinking about performing for thousands of viewers, but I didn't have a chance. After the meeting, we trouped over to Joy's house where Abby was waiting for us. Not only did we do our own parties, but Abby paid us to help her prepare and serve food at her catered events, too. Tonight was a combined Abby's Catering and Party Time event.

"Are you excited?" Linda Jean asked, as we entered the kitchen and put on our white aprons and hair nets.

"Definitely," Abby said. "This is the first time that Georgian School has asked a caterer outside the private school's staff to plan one of their orientations for the parents and the primary-school children. Having you girls there to entertain the children during the adult presentation will be very helpful."

"Maybe they'll book us for next year, too!" I exclaimed.

"Maybe they'll call us for every event that they plan during the school year!" Joy cried.

"Let's just get through this party," remarked Linda Jean. "We'll have to wait and see after that."

"That's smart thinking," Abby said. "But it doesn't hurt to look ahead. So, let's get to work and make the best pizza pinwheels ever."

Pizza Pinwheels are an Abby's Catering joke. Linda Jean accidentally spread pizza sauce and cheese on the cinnamon-roll dough during the first day of Abby's business. Instead of tasting terrible, the pizza pinwheels turned out to be delicious! Now they're our specialty. People who have tasted one ask to have them at their parties.

"What are we making today other than pizza pinwheels?" I asked.

Abby handed me the list of foods that we had to prepare for the afternoon party.

> *Guests expected—100 adults and*
> *50 children*
> *Pizza Pinwheels—4 batches*
> *Swirled deviled eggs—8 dozen*
> *Barbecued meatballs—12 dozen*
> *Cabbage rolls—12 dozen*
> *Salad bar*

"I'll roll the meatballs," I offered.

Joy said that she would make the deviled eggs. Linda Jean made the pizza pinwheels since she was so good at making them. Abby tackled the cabbage rolls, which were actually leaves of cabbage rolled up with rice and spices stuffed into them. Aimee cut up the salad bar fixings.

Abby flipped on the radio and set it on a fast-music station, and we got to work. Pretty soon we were dancing, chopping, singing, and laughing. We were having so much fun that I forgot my fears about the TV show.

We finished at one o'clock. There was plenty of time to take a swim, shower, and rest before the Georgian School orientation. It didn't start until four o'clock. I kept waiting for someone else to bring up the subject of the show, but no one did. I guess I was the only one who was nervous about being on television. Maybe working with the Georgian School students that night would take my mind off of being nervous.

We arrived at the school an hour early like we always did, so that we could set up our activity areas. The school sure didn't seem like any school that I had ever seen. It looked like an old mansion from the outside. There were even stables in back of the school!

"Wow, this place is fancy," I said as we entered the kitchen area. "Even the counters are beautiful!"

"The Georgian is one of the most exclusive private schools in Atlanta, and maybe in the whole state of Georgia," Abby told us. "Follow me into the auditorium. It's really fancy!"

Abby was right. The auditorium was fancy. It looked more like a plush movie theater than an auditorium.

"This would have been a good place to have the camera crew tape our show," Aimee said, looking all around.

"We sure would look ritzy!" Joy added. "I wish I had a place like this for practicing," she sighed, as she climbed the steps to the stage. "I think I'll bring the kids up one at a time to perform for the group." She jumped into the air and spun around. Then she made a mock curtsy to an imaginary audience.

I'd always envied Joy's ability to become a different person on stage. In fact, it was Joy who encouraged me to dress up as a clown and do my juggling and magic act for the school talent show last year. I won first place in the talent show, but I'm still convinced that it was because I knew that no one could see the real me under my makeup.

I don't know if I would have the courage to stand up as plain old Krissy Branch to do my act. At least I know that the kids like the clown.

"I'd better get into my outfit," I said, looking at the clock. Since there were going to be so many kids, we all planned to have stations that operated at the same time, with 12-15 children at each station. I was going to be performing my clown and magic act for two hours without a break.

My parents don't understand why I like being a clown so much. They don't understand much about me at all. I guess that's because Kitty is so famous. Because of that, it doesn't matter that I'm a straight-A student and that I was able to skip the third grade. It doesn't seem to matter that I'm first clarinet in the school band or that I'm the president of the computer club. My parents are always telling me to try harder.

"An education is the most important thing a person can have," my father tells me all the time.

"I was never very good in school," Mom

explained. "You shouldn't waste your intelligence."

They don't think that Kitty is wasting her intelligence by modeling and doing commercials. She's very important around our house. All I ever hear is, "Kitty this and Kitty that," and "Look at this latest magazine layout starring Kitty." She's made so much money that she will probably never have to go to college or get a job when she graduates from high school.

Being a clown is about the only thing that I do only for myself. Sometimes I just want to stop being smart, and I want to be funny. When I put on my red nose and white, pancake makeup, I'm not really me anymore. People expect me to act like a clown instead of a brain.

The Georgian students started filtering into the auditorium at 3:45 just as I was finishing my clown make-up. The first 15 minutes went well. I taught three kids how to juggle bean bags, and I did my scarf trick twice.

Out of the corner of my eye, I saw Linda Jean letting a cute, blond-haired girl pet her iguana. Aimee was gathering kids into a circle for games, and Joy was teaching her favorite dance that is called the One, Two, Hop, Hop, Hop! Suddenly, I realized that the party had turned into total chaos! More and more kids kept trailing in. There weren't 50 kids, as we had expected. There were at least 100!

Several babies started screaming. My hands were full of whining children. No one was paying attention to our directions. The noise level was terrible!

"Everyone who wants to watch the magic act, line up over here!" I shouted.

"Crafts are in this corner!" Aimee tried to yell over the crowd.

The auditorium looked like an ant hill with millions of squirming, shouting, confused ants swarming around without a queen.

"What are we going to do?" Linda Jean asked over the uproar.

"I don't know!" I shouted. "But I'm glad WBCC isn't filming this mess!"

"So, what's the deal?" a tall girl named Wendy asked. "Where's the great entertainment that I was promised? I could run this show better than you."

Joy sighed again and shook her head. "This is getting out of hand," she whispered to us.

"Wait! I have an idea that might save this

party." I tapped Wendy on the shoulder. "Do you really think you can do a better job than us?" I challenged, trying to look serious under my clown smile.

"Sure I can," she said, as she put her hands on her hips and stared at me.

"Yeah! Me, too! Just watch us!" yelled a boy named Robbie.

"We go to Georgian. We're the best!" shouted another boy.

"Okay, fine," I told them. "The kids are running the show now. You may use our supplies and the stage, and we'll be the guests."

"Really?" Wendy asked uncertainly.

"Yes, really," I turned my back on her and crossed my arms. "But if you don't think you can do it..." I waited to see if she would take my bait.

"No problem!" she said, as she stepped in front of me.

"We can do it," Robbie agreed.

By this time, most of the group was listening and waiting to see what our decision would be.

"Here's the deal," Aimee addressed the crowd.

Everyone became quiet to hear Aimee's

proposal. "You have 30 minutes to shape up. If you can't, then we want all of you to promise to follow our rules."

"We can do it in 15 minutes," Robbie boasted.

"We'll see," I said doubtfully. We took our seats in front of the stage. "Go ahead," I continued. "The clock is ticking."

The kids scrambled into planning huddles around the three leaders. We stared straight ahead and pretended not to care.

"Do you think it will work?" Joy asked.

"I hope so," I said. "They can't get much worse than they are now."

Three

OUR plan worked. Wendy, Robbie, and their friend Steve got the younger kids excited about putting on a show for us. We sat back and watched the kids take care of their own party for two hours, much longer than the expected 30 minutes.

We told Abby what happened on the ride home.

"I think you girls did a marvelous job of turning a potential crisis into a great day for the kids," Abby said.

"You should have seen this one little boy trying to dress up in Krissy's clown suit," Joy said. "He was so adorable! The sleeves hung down to his feet, and he had to roll the pants up about eight times."

"But he was good," I added. "He was one

of the ones I taught a few tricks to in the first few minutes before the mob showed up. He even did a fair job of juggling the bean bags. I was really impressed!"

"I really loved the talent contest," Aimee said. "Those two sisters with the matching outfits singing *On the Good Ship, Lollypop* were terrific. I laughed so hard I almost cried when they both fell on their bottoms."

Abby rounded the corner onto Honeybee Court and said, "I think one of Party Time's biggest assets is your ability to be flexible. Other entertainers might have kept trying to make things go as planned. By allowing the kids to put on the show, you saved the party."

Linda Jean nodded, and I could tell that she was thinking hard. "It worked this time, but what happens if something like this comes up while WBCC is filming? We don't want to be embarrassed on television."

I was thinking the same thing, but I wanted to seem optimistic. "It will be okay," I said as I got out of the car and helped unload the supplies. "I have a good feeling about our TV appearance."

Despite my worries, I headed home in high spirits. Things were going pretty well for me, after all. I was doing something special. I was a partner in a thriving business. I had come up with the idea that had saved the Georgian School party from becoming a disaster. I couldn't wait to tell my parents all about it.

"I'm home!" I called, walking in our front door.

"We're in the kitchen!" my dad called back.

Good, I thought. *Dad is home, too. I can tell everyone my news at the same time.* I hadn't told anyone in my family about my upcoming television appearance. I wanted to surprise the whole family when we were all together. I was sure Kitty would be amazed to find out that her big sister was going to be on TV just like she's been.

"Guess what, everyone," I said, as I entered the brightly lighted room. "The Forever Friends Club is going to be on *Weekend Mag* in two weeks. They're going to film our parties and interview us, and everything!"

"That's great, honey! Now we're going to have two stars in the family. Kitty just got a call from a director in Los Angeles. He saw her on the Corn Toasties cereal commercial, and he wants her to do a screen test for a movie! We all get to go to Los Angeles to watch

27

her do her screen test."

Kitty jumped up and hugged me. "Isn't it great? I'm going to be in a movie! You can ask me anything you want about performing in front of a camera. I can teach you, Aimee, Joy, and Linda Jean how to dress and do your makeup, and all that stuff. This is going to be lots of fun."

"Wait a minute! I didn't ask for a coach! I don't want my baby sister telling me what to do. In case you forgot, I'm very smart. I can figure it out all by myself. Go do your old movie. See if I care! They probably need someone to play the family dog."

"Krissy!" Mom gasped. "That wasn't very nice. I think that you should apologize to your sister."

"I'm sorry, Kitty," I said, even though I wasn't sorry for what I'd said.

"That's better. You should be happy for Kitty. She's young, but she has worked very hard to get as far as she has. It is the opportunity of a lifetime, even if she doesn't get the role," Dad said.

"I said I was sorry. I don't need a lecture." I turned and stomped out of the room. I could apologize later for mouthing off to dad, but right then I just needed to get out of that kitchen.

It never fails, I thought, as I hung up my clown suit in the closet and plopped down on my bed. *No matter what I do, Kitty beats me to it or does something better. I can play an instrument, but she can play two. I got my picture in the paper for rescuing a cat out from under a parked car when I was eight. Kitty had already had her picture in a hundred newspapers as the Squeezy Toilet Paper kid.*

Now I was going to be on TV, and I thought that I would be special for once. It was something that I had done on my own. And I wasn't going to be on TV for just a commercial or as just a model, but as a junior businesswoman. But Kitty was going to be a movie star, so my news meant nothing.

I went out into the hall and called Aimee.

"Lawrence residence," Aimee said when she picked up the phone.

"You beat your brothers to the phone. I'm shocked," I joked, trying not to hit her with all my problems right away.

"It was easy," she laughed with me. "I tied up all four of them in the living room."

"Did you really?" I asked.

"No, they were all at Randy's soccer game when I came home. There was a note on the refrigerator about heating up burritos for dinner," Aimee said.

"That sounds good. Do you want some company?" I asked.

"Is there trouble at home?" Aimee asked.

"Yeah, I'll tell you about it when I get there," I said.

I left a note on my bed and went out the sliding glass door that connects my room to the backyard. I went through a gate into Aimee's yard and met her at the back door.

"What's going on?" she asked, even before I sat down at the table. Aimee was used to the Branch family saga. Of all my friends, she was the one I told my troubles to the most.

"Kitty is going to be a movie star," I told her. "We're all going to Los Angeles for her screen test. I can hardly wait," I said sarcastically.

"I thought having brothers was tough!" Aimee sympathized.

I shook my head. "She just never quits! I thought she'd lose her charm and good looks when she lost her teeth, but the photographers think she's adorable—gap and all."

"Relax. Maybe she'll get fat when she becomes a teenager," Aimee said, trying to make me feel better.

"I doubt it. Look at me. Look at my mother and father. We're all thin as rails."

"Well, you can always hope that she gets zits or something," Aimee said.

"Then they would use her for zit medicine commercials. Aimee, it's hopeless," I said, picking at my burrito.

We ate in silence. I was worrying about Kitty's fame and popularity, and Aimee allowed me to just wallow in my misery. As we finished our drinks, the phone rang, and Aimee reached up to answer it.

"Hello," Aimee answered the phone. "Oh, hi, Abby. Sure, we'll do it. We'll be right over."

"What was that all about?" I asked.

"Abby's waiting for Mr. Marshall to call, and she has to deliver a box of pita bread sandwiches to the mid-summer faculty meeting at the junior high. I told her that we'd take the sandwiches over to the school on our bikes."

"Maybe a bike ride will clear my head. I'll call my parents and tell them where I'm going. I doubt they even know I'm gone," I said.

I got permission from my parents to ride

over to the school, apologized again for my earlier behavior, and got my bike out of the garage. Aimee and I picked up the box of sandwiches at Abby's and strapped it to the rack on the back of Aimee's bike.

"The teachers will be in the faculty lounge on the first floor of the main building," Abby told us. "They're expecting you, so the doors will be open."

"I wonder if we'll get to meet our teachers for next year?" I asked.

"They aren't supposed to post the class assignments until August, but maybe they would tell us if we asked?" Aimee wondered. "On top of everything else, you're not getting nervous about school next year, are you?"

Once again, Aimee had zeroed in on another of my nagging problems. Last year I was in seventh grade, and the rest of the Forever Friends Club were in sixth grade. That meant they were in a different building from me. And this year I'll be in eighth grade, and they'll all be in seventh grade. It will be weird. I mean, it will be neat to be in the same building with them, but at the same time, I was kind of used to being on my own. I had my own group to eat lunch with and to hang out with between classes. And last year all the seventh graders thought that the eighth graders were snobs. I hoped that the other members of the Forever Friends Club wouldn't include me in that category.

We turned the corner on Locust, and we continued until we got to Martin Luther King Junior High School. "Don't worry," Aimee said. "We'll all get along great at school this fall!" That was the weird thing about Aimee. She always seemed to read my mind.

"I know that. It's hard to explain exactly how I feel," I sighed. "Remember how snobby and bossy I thought the eighth graders were last year? I just don't want you to think that I'm going to be that way."

We parked and locked our bikes to the rack. Aimee gave me a quick hug. "We would never think that."

Aimee carried the box of pita sandwiches, and I held the door open for her. We found the teachers in the lounge having their mid-summer planning meeting.

My teacher for the seventh grade, Mrs. Wright, greeted us. "Hello, Krissy. Hello, Aimee. You girls are just in time with the food. We're all really hungry around here."

The other teachers around the room nodded and voiced their agreement. Those that knew us said hello.

"These will fill you up. Abby's catering guarantees it," Aimee said, smiling and handing her the box.

"How are your summers going?" Mrs. Byrd asked. "Mrs. Marshall says that you've started a business with some of your friends. That's very ambitious, if you ask me."

"Yes, our business is called Party Time. We work for Abby's Catering, and we plan parties for younger children on the side," I said.

"How is it going so far?" asked Mrs. Wright.

"We've already done 11 parties," Aimee answered. "We really like working with the kids."

"That's great, girls. Now, I don't suppose you girls would like to find out ahead of time who your homeroom teachers will be next year, would you?" Mrs. Wright asked, changing the subject.

"Well, sure," I said, hesitating a little.

"As it happens, we just finished making the class lists, so we have the information right here." Mrs. Wright picked up a large chart off the table. "Hmmm, let me see. I know that

Aimee is in my class. And, Krissy, you have Mr. Paulo for both homeroom and algebra." She looked up at us and smiled. "I hope that's okay with you!"

"That sounds great!" Aimee said with enthusiasm.

"Yeah," I echoed.

"Let me introduce you to Mr. Paulo," Mrs. Wright said. A tall, dark-haired man rose from the seat by the window and shook my hand.

"I've been hearing fantastic things about you, Kristina," he said while shaking my hand. "I'm looking forward to a productive year."

"It's nice to meet you," I said quietly. "I'll do my best."

"I'm counting on you to get the older kids to work harder," he said.

"I'd rather not be singled out," I said. "It's hard enough to fit in as it is."

He grinned and stopped shaking my hand. "You're even smarter than I thought!" he exclaimed. "I'll see you in September, and get ready to work hard."

Aimee and I said good-bye and left the teachers to their sandwiches and plans.

"I can't believe it," I told Aimee when we reached our bikes. "Mr. Paulo is the hardest teacher in the school. Last year 16 people flunked his homeroom.

"They flunked homeroom? How can you flunk homeroom? All you do is show up and listen to announcements over the loud-speaker."

"It's because they were tardy so many times," I told her. "In Mr. Paulo's class, if you get five tardies, you get an *F*."

"Wow," Aimee said.

"Yeah, wow! If he's like that in homeroom, can you imagine what he's like as an algebra teacher?" I asked. "I hope he doesn't really want to use me as an example for the other students. They resent me enough already for being a year younger than they are. First Kitty, and now this. What a day!"

Four

I woke up the next morning feeling a little better. I decided that it wouldn't kill me to be nice to my family. Maybe they'd even notice it and stop treating me like a second-class citizen compared to Kitty.

By the time they all got out of bed, I had bacon, eggs, and hashbrowns sizzling on the stove. I used the electric juice maker to squeeze fresh orange juice, and I baked a batch of bran muffins.

Kitty walked into the kitchen first. "Mmmm, something smells good," she said. "Do you want some help?"

"Sure," I said, thinking that my plan to overwhelm my family with kindness was already working. "You can set the table and slice up this apple while I watch the eggs. Are

Mom and Dad on their way?"

"I passed them in the hall. They said they'd be here in a minute," Kitty reported.

My parents walked into the kitchen just as Kitty was finishing setting the table. "Krissy, this is fantastic," Mom said. "I wasn't going to have time to fix breakfast before going to work this morning. This is definitely better than grabbing something at the cafeteria."

"It's healthier, too!" Dad added. "I guess all of your experience with Abby's Catering is paying off!"

I smiled. My plan was working perfectly. "Why don't you sit down? The hashbrowns are almost ready."

"Sit here, Mom, Dad," I heard Kitty say. "I set these places just for you. See the neat way I folded your napkins like little hats? I learned that in school."

"That's very nice, Kitty," Dad commented.

"And here are the apples that I sliced," Kitty went on fishing for compliments. "I didn't cut my fingers or anything."

"Good job," Mom said.

I was burning up inside. *Kitty always has to grab the spotlight,* I thought. She was so sweet when she asked if she could help. I

38

wouldn't have let her help if I had known that this was going to happen. All of a sudden, I was in a bad mood. I didn't even smile when I handed my parents their plates and they told me how appetizing everything looked. Kitty had already ruined breakfast for me.

Not only that, but she spent the next 15 minutes talking all about the trip to Los Angeles.

"May I stay here when you go out to Los Angeles?" I asked when I could finally get a word in edgewise. "I'm sure that Party Time will have several parties to do, and—"

"Come on, Kristina," Dad said. "Who can turn down a trip to Los Angeles? It'll be a great family trip. We'll go to your sister's screen test, and maybe we'll even have a little time to do some sightseeing. You might even see a movie star or two! You don't want to miss that to stay here and be a clown, do you?"

Yes, I did. I really did.

"No, I guess not," I told him. Inside I was screaming, *You don't care about me and what I want. All you think about is Kitty, Kitty, Kitty!* And speaking of Kitty, she was talking again.

"You know, Krissy," she said in a snobby tone, "it's like I told you before. I could give you and your friends a lot of advice about how to look and act in front of a camera. I know about lights and shadows, and what kinds of clothes show up best."

"No, thanks," I gritted out between clenched teeth. "We don't need your help."

"You really should think about taking Kitty up on her offer," Mom said. "She has had much more experience than the four of you at getting her picture taken."

"Aimee's father can tell us what to do. He works in front of the camera every day." I wanted to mention the every day bit because Kitty didn't appear on television that often, and it was always taped, not live like the news.

"Yes, I'm sure Gerald Lawrence will help you all he can. But he is a busy man," Dad reminded me. "Kitty will be a big help on the details."

Kitty finished her breakfast and jumped up to clear the table. "You just let me know when the sessions are, and I'll go to the station with you. I'll be your personal wardrobe and makeup consultant."

"I have to go to work now," I said, getting up and deliberately leaving my plate and glass on the table. *If Kitty is so determined to show off,* I thought, *then let her!* I had to get out of there before I blew my cool. There was no way that I was going to let Kitty come to the station and give me advice—no way at all!

* * * * *

"Can you believe her?" I asked my friends later when we were at Joy's house. "She actually insists on being our makeup and wardrobe consultant! And, of course, Mom and Dad think it's a great idea."

I grabbed a pillow off the couch and screamed into it.

"Don't worry," Aimee assured me. "We'll schedule the tapings when Kitty's busy."

"That way she won't be able to come, but it won't look like it's on purpose," agreed Joy.

"Doesn't Kitty have a pretty full schedule with acting and dance lessons, and photo sessions?" asked Linda Jean.

I started feeling a little better. "That's true. She's hardly ever home. I'm sure we can fix it so that we tape the show on days she will be busy."

Joy shrugged her shoulders. "We'll just say, 'Sorry, Kitty. It just can't be helped.'"

We all laughed, and I started feeling better again. I could always count on the Forever Friends Club to lift my spirits.

"So, let's get down to business," Aimee said. "We have two parties this week and two next week. The unicorn and magic party for Shannon Kellar is on Thursday, and the outdoor cookout for Brandon Kenneth is on Friday. The 'teddy bears are people, too' theme for May Solomon is next Thursday. It's a good thing you'll only be in Los Angeles for a couple of days, Krissy. We're going to need all the help we can get!"

"Which ones should we tell my dad about?" Aimee asked. "I think we could do something really special for the unicorns and magic party."

"Cookouts are always fun, and teddy bears are popular. Why don't we tell him about all three?" Joy suggested.

Abby walked into the living room at that moment and sat down to help us decide. "What would you like to do in the way of food for the unicorn party? I haven't made the cake for that party yet, so we could do something really special for that."

"How about rainbow parfaits with frozen

yogurt and fresh fruit?" I asked. "That would go along with the theme. When I think of unicorns, I imagine fluffy clouds, moonlit nights, and crystal clear lakes."

"Hmmm," Abby murmured. "I like the idea of a lake. Let's go into the kitchen and see what ideas are in the cake decorating book," Abby said.

We all trouped into the kitchen and paged through the huge book. Each page was like a ticket to a fairy tale. There were characters from nursery rhymes, dragons, baseball hats, and wedding couples. The trouble was that we liked a part of all the ideas.

Abby ended up drawing a design for the cake with a waterfall and a family of unicorns standing in the reflecting pool at the bottom of the waterfall. The pool would actually be a mirror. Then Abby drew a forest with sparkling trees that had Christmas tree icicles dangling from the leaves. "It's beautiful," Joy told her, and we all murmured our agreement.

"It's a good thing that we have plenty of time to prepare for this party," Abby said, smiling. Then she sent us off to find the icicles and the plastic models of unicorns that she would cover with sugar.

As soon as we had collected the decorations for the cake, we sat down to make a list of needed supplies and a schedule.

1:00 P.M.— Arrive at Shannon Kellar's house. Set up the activities.

1:15 P.M.— Decorate the dining room with pink, silver, and white streamers.

1:30 P.M.— Show the camera people around.

1:45 P.M.— Joy and Krissy dress. Aimee and Linda Jean pass out the name tags as the children begin to arrive.

2:00 P.M.— Clown act: Krissy

2:30 P.M.— Crafts: Aimee

2:45 P.M.— Dance: Joy

3:00 P.M.— Cake and presents: all

3:30 P.M.— Science: Linda Jean

3:45 P.M.— Songs until the parents come to pick up the children: Aimee leading, and all join in.

4:00 P.M.— Cleaning up after the party: all

"We can't plan this party too carefully," Linda Jean said. "It has to be perfect."

My stomach started to feel funny again as

I thought about trying to perform while controlling the kids in front of a camera.

"What if it isn't perfect?" I worried. "The last two parties have been near disasters. What if this one turns out the same way?"

"It won't," Joy said confidently, "because we're going to memorize every detail. Nothing could possibly go wrong this time."

Five

WE arrived at the Kellar's house at 1:00 P.M. to set up. Abby's unicorn cake was magnificent. She set it on the silver and white tablecloth that covered the table in the dining room. We hung a canopy of silver, white, and pink crepe-paper streamers above the table. The streamers twisted from the center of the light out to the corners of the room.

"It's so beautiful!" Shannon Kellar cried when she walked into the room a few minutes later. Shannon's pink-lace birthday dress went perfectly with the fairy-tale atmosphere of the room. "When will the television people be here?" she asked. "It's so neat that my party is going to be on TV. I can't wait!"

"Well, we'll have to wait a little bit. The camera crew said that they would get here

about 15 minutes before the kids were scheduled to arrive," I told her. "Would you like to
help us set up the games?" I asked Shannon.

"First I have to take Big Tom out to the
backyard," said Shannon.

"Who's Big Tom?" Linda Jean asked.

"Our Great Dane," said Shannon. "Most
of the time he plays in the house, but Mom
said that he shouldn't come to the party."

"That's a great idea," Linda Jean said,
laughing.

I glanced sideways at her and rolled my
eyes. "That's just what we need, a dog as big
as a horse at the party."

"We could strap a horn on him and call
him a unicorn," Aimee joked.

"That's not funny!" Joy and I both said at
once.

"Don't be so serious, you guys," Aimee said.
"Remember that this is just a local show."

"That's right! It's a local show that everyone in Atlanta watches. A little TV appearance that is probably going to change our
lives," I said. "Does my hair look okay?"

"What does it matter? You're going to cover
it with a wig, anyway?" Aimee reminded me.

"Oh, right," I said, forcing a smile. I could

feel myself getting nervous, but I tried to keep busy and to keep smiling. I managed to smile at the camera crew when they arrived, but I knew it was a fake smile. As soon as the introductions were finished, I ran to the bathroom to put on my clown outfit.

I looked at my watch. We were five minutes behind schedule. I quickly patted on my makeup and strapped on my nose. I was sweating so much by the time I finally wrestled my new silver and white wig onto my head that I had to pat more white powder onto my face to cover the streaks.

Joy came in to make sure that her new dance outfit was all in place. I told her that she looked beautiful, and comfortable in her sleeveless leotard and skirt.

"You look great, too, Krissy," Joy said. "The kids are going to love all the tinsel that you sewed onto your outfit. And the wig is perfect."

"I wish it felt perfect. I'm about to die from the heat, and I'm sick to my stomach. Maybe I'm getting the flu. Maybe I need to eat something," I said.

"It's probably just stage fright," Joy explained. "I get it every time I have to dance in a recital. It's good for you. It makes you perform better on stage."

"All it's doing for me right now is making me sick. I wonder how Kitty does it? She always looks like she's enjoying herself in front of the camera."

"She's used to it for one thing," Joy said. "Just think of how much fun you had at the talent show at school last year, and all the performances you've given for kids at parties. You love being the center of attention. Remember how good you are, and forget about the cameras."

"You're right. No one knows who I am under this face, anyway," I joked weakly.

Feeling a little better, I walked out to the living room. Linda Jean and Aimee had put name tags on all the kids as we were getting dressed. *It's too bad they didn't put leashes on them, too!* I thought. The kids were running around all over the place, and they seemed to be under the camera crew's feet constantly. I looked at my watch. I took a deep breath and watched the camera swing toward me.

Out of my huge side pockets I pulled two sets of silver bells. I held up my hands and rang the bells. *So far, so good,* I thought. The kids looked toward me, and I let the bells slide down into my sleeves.

"Where did they go?" Shannon asked, moving through the crowd of kids to stand by me.

"It's magic," I replied. "They disappeared." Then I started wiggling around and letting the bells make noise inside my shirt.

"She put them in her shirt!" a boy named Ricky shouted. "I can hear them!"

"Oooh!" I jumped and shook. "Ahhh!" I wiggled and rang the bells as they traveled the length of my outfit to my feet. "I tell you, it's magic. The bells are gone." I opened my eyes wide and pretended to look innocent. "Don't you believe me?"

"No!" they all shouted.

The kids thought my act was great. They knew I had the bells, but they thought I was trying to fool them into thinking that the bells were gone. By the time the bells fell out onto the floor, every kid in the room was laughing.

"That wasn't a very good trick," Ricky said.

"Okay," I said, using my favorite line. "You try it."

While the group looked on, I went around behind Ricky and pretended to drop the bells in his shirt. I stood behind him and shook him as I rubbed the bells down his back to his feet. Before anyone noticed, I dropped them into my secret pocket and stood up.

"Well, where are they?" I asked sweetly.

Ricky shook and shook, but the bells wouldn't come out.

"Congratulations!" I cheered, shaking his hand. "I've been trying that trick for weeks and have never been able to do it as well as you did the first time."

Ricky smiled and bowed to the audience. As he walked back to join them, I tapped him on the shoulder. "Uh, Ricky," I whispered loud enough for the group to hear. "I need my bells back before I leave, okay?"

I went on to my next trick before the shocked expression left Ricky's face.

I was enjoying myself so much that I *almost* forgot about the camera. Aimee came in to guide the kids over to the craft tables that were set up outside. Things were going well and only slightly behind schedule—until the dog got in.

Just as Aimee opened the patio door to let the kids file out with the camera person in tow, Big Tom streaked past us and headed straight for the dining room. Mrs. Kellar yelled at him, but he ran right past her. I jumped to catch him, but I missed.

Big Tom didn't miss the cake, though. He stood up on his hind legs and put his front paws right on top of the waterfall.

Shannon screamed. Abby just sat down and stared numbly at the ruined masterpiece.

The cameraperson said, "Oh, I wish I had taken a shot of the cake earlier."

We all looked at each other and almost cried. "Two days of work for nothing," Joy said.

"They didn't even get a picture of it before it was smashed," Linda Jean said. I grabbed Big Tom by the collar and hauled him outside. I was so upset that I didn't even bother to say, "Bad dog."

From then on the kids went wild. We had to yell at them a lot, which is something that we never have to do. Misbehaving was the norm rather than the exception that day. The camera crew gave up and rescheduled for Brandon Kenneth's party the next day.

We managed to pull the party back together by the end. Aimee even made up a dog-in-the-cake song, but it was too late to salvage the filming. This was the first time we left a party and weren't able to even smile about the mishaps. I felt awful and so did everyone else.

*   *   *   *   *

I won't go into details, but Brandon Kenneth's party was worse. I told my parents the sad story over dinner the next night. It was a relief to spill out my anger to someone.

"I can't believe that Shannon Kellar didn't at least tie up that huge dog. Who lets a Great Dane run loose inside the house, anyway? He just wags his tail and wipes all the dishes off the table!" I exclaimed.

I was glad that Kitty wasn't there to hear my failures.

"And Brandon Kenneth's friends were the worst!" I went on. "One of them actually started a fire on the kitchen counter by sneaking a piece of charcoal out of the barbecue pit. Some cookout," I added. "The boys were so busy throwing food at each other and trying to add dirty words to the camp songs that I couldn't have done my magic act even if someone hadn't stolen my bag of tricks and hidden it in the shed."

"It sounds like it was pretty bad," Mom

agreed. "Maybe having a camera crew around makes the kids act differently."

"I doubt it. I think Brandon's friends have been brats for a long time," I said.

"This doesn't sound like you at all," Dad said. "You love little kids. You're always talking about how cute they are, even when they're bratty!"

"Oh, I don't know," I said, rubbing my temples with my fingertips. "I guess we're all worried about looking good for this television show. None of us are acting like ourselves."

"I told you so! You should have listened to me," Kitty said, stepping out from behind the kitchen door.

"How long have you been spying on me?" I demanded. *That's the last straw,* I thought. *I can't even have a private conversation with my parents without Kitty sticking her nose in!*

"Oh, I've been here long enough to know that you really do need my help!" Kitty announced.

I tossed my head back and took a bite of salad, chewing slowly.

"No, thanks, Kitty. We'll manage!" I cried.

"Yeah, you'll manage to get your show

canceled and lose all your business," Kitty said.

"What makes you so smart? You weren't even there. You don't know anything about it. And you're only nine years old. I'm not taking advice from a baby."

"Okay, that's enough, girls!" Dad raised his voice. "It's not going to do any good to argue. Krissy, you need help, and Kitty is willing to give it to you. It wouldn't hurt you to listen to her."

I went back to eating my salad in silence. I didn't agree to listen. I did plan to watch Kitty's screen test very carefully and take notes, though. The next filming of us doing a party wasn't scheduled to take place until next week. In the meantime, the Branch family was going to Los Angeles.

Six

I didn't get a chance to see Aimee, Joy, or Linda Jean again before we left on Monday for Los Angeles. I did talk to Aimee on the phone, though. I told her my plan to take notes at Kitty's screen test.

"That sounds like a really good idea," Aimee said. "I don't know what's gone wrong lately, but we'd better do something about it fast. Joy said that Mr. Baxter called to cancel a party after he heard what had happened at Brandon's house."

"That's bad," I said. "If the parties keep getting out of control like they have been lately, we'll lose all our business!"

"Luckily, Joy was able to talk him out of canceling. She said we'd give him a money-back guarantee so that if he wasn't satisfied, he could get his money back." Aimee said.

"That was good thinking. Well, I have to get going now. Dad's honking the horn for me to hurry up. I'll let you know what I find out in Los Angeles," I assured Aimee.

"Have a good trip," Aimee said.

As we rode in the car to the airport and boarded the airplane for Los Angeles, I kept telling myself to be nice to my sister. It wasn't very hard to do, because she barely talked to me during the entire trip.

As soon as we got on the plane, Kitty started to turn on her charm. She made friends with all the flight attendants. She even managed to get invited up to the cockpit to visit with the pilot. The attendant asked me along, too, but I pretended to be asleep. I realized later that I should have gone, if only to watch Kitty. She really knows how to stand out in a group.

During band and computer club, I don't have to be very outgoing and friendly. I just have to do my job and be smart. The same goes for getting good grades. It's okay to act crazy when people expect me to, and hiding behind my makeup makes it easy.

I was so busy thinking about all the times I have tried not to be singled out of a group that I almost missed the view of downtown

Los Angeles as we flew into the airport.

A limousine met us at the airport. The driver took the long way to the movie studio so that we could see some of the sights on the way. It would probably be the only time that we would have to sightsee. Our schedule was pretty full, with Kitty's screen test and all the other stuff that she had to do.

The front of the studio was fancy. It had huge trees, columns, arches, and ornate windows. But after we drove through the gates to the studio, the scenery changed. The streets looked like any other streets, and the buildings were ordinary. I didn't see any famous movie stars walking around like I thought I would.

We pulled up in front of Sound Stage Number Six. We were greeted at the door by Ms. Fairchild. She is Kitty's agent, the person who schedules jobs for Kitty.

"Welcome to Los Angeles," she said. "We have time for a short tour of the studio before your screen test," she said to Kitty and then looked at Mom and Dad for their approval.

"I thought you'd never ask!" Mom shrieked. "I'm dying to get an insider's glimpse of some of my favorite TV shows!"

Dad laughed. "I'd just like to have a look around."

No one asked me. I tagged along, poking my head around corners and trying to see through windows. I saw mostly narrow alleys and offices.

I wasn't really impressed until we actually entered a set where filming was taking place. On the stage there were actors I had seen on one of my favorite situation comedies. Bert Middleman, Connie Throng, and Jep Jep, the dog, were actually there in person. They were talking (or barking) to each other and the crew as if they were real people!

They are real, I reminded myself. But it was hard not to stare.

The equipment was even more impressive. There were lights, cameras, and people with props everywhere. At first, it looked very confusing. But as I watched more closely, it became obvious that each person had a specific job. I wondered if Mr. Lawrence's studio was as busy and hectic as this one was.

"All right, Kitty," Ms. Fairchild said at last. "Are you ready to see the set where you'll be testing for the part?"

"I've been ready since you called last week!"

Kitty squealed. "This is the most exciting thing I've ever done! Do you think we can meet Alissa Toole? She's my favorite."

Ms. Fairchild smiled. "I'm sure that can be arranged."

That's another difference between me and Kitty. I would never have had the nerve to ask to meet a star, even if the star was only 10 years old like Alissa Toole was. *Kitty is either very brave or very naive,* I thought.

Whatever she is, people instantly like her.

We walked outside, down an alley, past a cafeteria where I was sure I saw Katheryn M. Shaw eating soup, and into another building.

"Screen tests aren't nearly as wild as the taping of a comedy like the one you just saw," Ms. Fairchild explained as we walked down a flight of stairs and emerged on a tiny stage. A large screen sat in the background with a picture of a harbor that was filled with sailboats and ships anchored in the distance. In front of the screen was a wooden pier, a bait shack, and an overturned rowboat with a hole in the bottom of it. Sand crunched under our feet as we walked.

"Michael, this is Kitty Branch. These are her parents, William and Jillian Branch. And this is her sister, Kristina," Ms. Fairchild said. "This is Michael Drake, the casting director for Castaway Island, the movie that Kitty is testing for."

Kitty stepped forward and handed Mr. Drake her portfolio, a collection of her modeling photographs. She shook his hand. "Thank you for inviting us, Mr. Drake. I appreciate the chance to test for the part, and I look forward to working with you."

This didn't sound like the whiny, attention-grabbing Kitty that lived at our house. This was Kitty the Professional. Kitty had an attitude that said *of course, I'll get the job.* I guess I hadn't noticed it before because, frankly, I hadn't cared.

"Step this way," Mr. Drake instructed. "Have you had a chance to read the script that I sent you?"

"I've read it about a hundred times!" Kitty enthused. "I love the character of Mary. She's a lot like me."

Michael Drake laughed. "Maybe she is at that." I could see that he was impressed already.

Mom, Dad, Ms. Fairchild, and I sat in folding chairs away from the set and watched as a makeup person applied blusher to Kitty's cheeks and combed her hair.

"First, let's read the scene that I circled in red. I'll play the part of the fisherman."

Kitty had her part memorized. She climbed up on the wooden piling and dangled her feet over the imaginary water. From where we were sitting it looked like real water because of the movie running on the screen behind her.

I couldn't take my eyes off Kitty. She was totally an actress. Soon, I knew, I wouldn't have a sister who was just a famous model to deal with. Kitty was good enough to really be a star one day. That thought didn't make me as mad as I thought it would. In fact, I found myself silently cheering on Kitty as she acted out her role on camera.

Then Mr. Drake abruptly stopped the test and looked hard at Kitty. I held my breath.

"Good job, Kitty. Turn to page 28, and look at the top," instructed Mr. Drake.

Kitty quickly flipped to the page that he indicated and began reading. In a second, she put the script down and jumped off the pier onto the fake beach.

Pick up the script, I thought, but I didn't need to worry. Kitty had memorized that scene, too, and every other scene that Michael Drake had her read.

"How does she do that?" I whispered to Mom.

"I don't know," Mom answered. "But memorizing comes easily for her."

"I guess so," I said.

When the test was over, the cameraman ran the videotape back so that we could see the scene with the background attached.

"You really look like you're at the ocean," I told her. "You did a good job. I learned a lot," I admitted.

"Thanks," Kitty said, still smiling from ear to ear. "Let's go eat. I'm starved."

The grown-ups laughed. "At least Kitty knows what her priorities are," Mr. Drake joked. "Food is an excellent idea. I'll treat you to the commissary. That's where all the famous and the soon-to-be-famous stars eat."

"Do they have hamburgers?" Kitty asked.

Ms. Fairchild opened the door to let us pass through. "They have whatever you want, Kitty."

I could tell by the way Ms. Fairchild and Mr. Drake were looking at each other that they were happy with Kitty's performance. I found myself feeling happy for Kitty. That was a new experience.

What I needed, I decided after watching Kitty charm and capture the hearts of everyone in the studio commissary, was a little bit of Kitty's confidence. She always acts as if life is going to go her way, and it usually does.

She expects to be treated like a miniature adult, and she is treated that way. She isn't pushy or snobby about it. At least away from home she isn't! Kitty is a friendly person who seems to like everyone, and people instantly like her in return. Maybe I have been wrong about her being snobby. Maybe I've felt ignored because I've been jealous.

I ate and talked with the group at lunch. I managed to shake hands with a movie star or two. I met Alissa Toole, who in person was just like any other kid we gave parties for. I told her about Party Time, and she actually said that she wished she lived in Atlanta so that we could do a party for her! That made me feel good.

By the time lunch was over, I was feeling pretty good about myself, about Kitty, and about the upcoming television debut of Party Time. *If only I could maintain this attitude when I get home,* I thought.

That night I started writing a journal in a spiral notebook that I brought with me on the trip. I decided not to think only about improving my outlook on life, but to write down my decisions and feelings on paper, too.

I took my pen out and wrote:

1. *Stop trying to outdo Kitty.*
2. *Drop clubs that I don't care about,*
   and concentrate on only one or two
   activities.
3. *Be happy.*
4. *Be a better big sister.*

That seemed like enough to work on for one night. I put my notebook away and climbed into the big hotel bed. I fell asleep thinking about doing a television talk show with Kitty.

"Yes," I would tell the interviewer, "Kitty got her start in modeling, and I got my start as a clown. Both of us are fabulously happy. Yes, it's simply marvelous."

Seven

WE were back in Atlanta before we knew it. It was great to see my friends again, but we still had to worry about doing well on the television show.

"All I know is that we have to stop letting this TV show interfere with our parties," I said to Aimee, Joy, and Linda Jean as we walked along the bike path at the university the day after I got back from Los Angeles. "Not only are we close to ruining our chances at even being on the show, but we are going to start losing business!"

"She's right," Aimee said. "We've really let this show business stuff get out of hand. I never thought I could act like such a fool in front of the camera."

"I never thought I would yell right at a kid

because he ruined my chances at stardom," Joy added. "I can't believe the things I said in front of Shannon when her dog wrecked the cake. I was just so mad because of all the work we'd done. If I'd been thinking clearly, I would have made sure that Big Tom was tied up before the party started."

"I would have, too," said Linda Jean. "If I had had one brain in my head that day, I would have realized that Shannon wasn't gone long enough to tie him up securely."

"If only we weren't so busy worrying about what we looked like or how we sounded, or all the kids making us look good," I continued. "Every time I think about it, I want to kick myself!"

"What are we going to do?" Linda Jean asked. "Ever since Josh's party, it has been one mess after another. First the Georgian School, then Shannon's and Brandon's parties. The kids seem to be misbehaving more than usual."

I snapped my fingers. "The problem is concentration," I told them. "I decided over the weekend that next year I wouldn't join so many clubs and get burned out. I'm going to concentrate on Party Time and band. I'm going to stop worrying about whether a teacher singles me out as an example for the class. I'm going to just be myself."

"That's great, Krissy. But how will that advice help us?" Linda Jean asked.

"Because we need to do the same thing. We need to concentrate," I said.

Aimee turned around and walked backward in front of us. "Krissy is onto something, you guys. We need to concentrate on the kids and on helping them have a good time. We need to pay attention to them, not to ourselves or the cameras. This television business is only going to last another week, but Party Time is going to go on for a long time. It would be better to cancel the show than ruin our business."

Aimee's speech made sense. We decided that we really didn't want to have to cancel the show, but if it came to a choice, we would choose Party Time over our one hour of fame.

"Do you think that we should refund the Kellars' and the Kenneths' money?" Joy asked. "After all, they probably weren't satisfied."

"I think we should," I said, turning on my heel and heading back home at a fast pace. "Let's call them and apologize right now. We'll offer to return their money."

We practically knocked each other over, running back to Joy's house to phone our clients. I felt a surge of hope as we ran through the wooded paths together. The Forever Friends Club would make it right.

Later that evening, I was writing down what had happened in my new journal. It turned out that the Kellars and the Kenneths didn't want their money back, so we agreed to do the next party that they wanted for free. It was only fair, Aimee told them, since they had been nice enough to open their homes to the TV people and their parties had turned out to be less than satisfactory because of the TV people.

I heard a knock on my door just as I was putting away my journal. "Who is it?" I called.

"It's Kitty. Can I talk to you a minute?"

"Sure, come on in." I wasn't even sure why I said that or why I had invited Kitty into my room. I hadn't done that in a long time. But I've felt differently toward Kitty since our weekend in Los Angeles. I sort of had more respect for her career.

She peeked around the door to see if I had really said for her to come in.

I motioned for her to come inside and sit

on my bed with me. "What's up?" I asked.

"I didn't get the job," she said quickly. "Mr. Drake just called. He said they found a 13 year old who is small enough to play a nine year old." She started crying. "I tried my best, Krissy. I really did."

"I know you did, Kitty." I put my arm around her and let her cry on my shoulder. "I thought you did a great job. I was really impressed."

"You were?" she sniffled. "I thought you hated me. I thought you hated my modeling and the commercials I did."

"I don't hate it," I said. "Well, maybe I do resent it a little. But, I would have been proud of you if you had gotten the part."

"Mr. Drake said my screen test looked good and that he was going to keep it, in case another part for someone my age comes up."

I handed her a tissue. "See, it's not so bad after all. You'll be a star one day."

"But, I really wanted this part. I was so nervous before I started reading. The whole time they were filming I thought I would choke."

"You were nervous?" I asked incredulously. "You sure didn't look it! I've always admired that about you. You get along so well with people. You just charge right into a situation or a room and light it up. I always hang back and wait for someone else to make the first move."

Kitty studied me for a moment. "That's not true. You're so smart. Mom and Dad are always telling me to try my best in school, but I'll never be as smart as you are. They say that if I try harder, I can have grades that are just as good as yours and that I can be in the band and the computer club if I want to."

"Do you want to?" I asked, still thinking about what she had said. I never knew that my parents noticed all the things I do. I certainly never thought that they used me as an example for Kitty to follow. *If anything, it was the other way around,* I thought. "Do you want to be in the band and the computer club?" I asked again.

Kitty shook her head. "No, I want to be a model and an actress for awhile. I don't know what I want to be when I grow up."

"That's strange. I thought you wanted to be a star," I said.

Kitty finally cracked a smile. "Mom and Dad want me to be a star. I'm thinking of going out for soccer."

"Soccer! Won't you ruin your picture-perfect knees?"

She laughed and then said seriously, "I want to see if I'm good at something other than having my picture taken."

"Then I think you should give it a try. I'll come to your games," I assured her.

"Thanks," she said gratefully.

We sat on the bed and retied the bows that held the squares of my patchwork quilt together at the corners. This was a side of Kitty that I had never seen before. She seemed less sure of herself. Maybe I could ask for advice from her, after all.

"So, what were those tips you were going to give me? We could really use your help," I said.

Kitty's eyes lighted up. "Really? I'm not trying to boss you around, you know."

"I know," I said.

She jumped off the bed and paced back and forth across the room. "The first thing you have to do is imagine a curtain between you and the camera. Pretend that it's a black curtain that you can't see or hear through. You pretend that all the commotion is happening to a different person."

"Okay, then what?" I asked eagerly.

"Remember that if you blow your lines, they'll just shoot another take. They want the show to be a success as much as you do. If you look good, then they look good."

"You sound more like an adult than a kid," I told her.

"I've heard this stuff enough times. I've memorized it just like my lines," she said.

"How do I act like myself when they shove that camera so close? I was trying to do a trick the other day, and the guy's zoom lens was almost touching my nose."

"Laugh," Kitty said.

"Laugh?" I asked.

"Yes, laugh. You're a clown, right? Then laugh. Laughing makes the butterflies and the stage fright go away. When I was doing the cereal commercial last month, they wanted to take a picture of my eye winking. They put the camera practically on my cheek. I laughed. and then I imagined that I was in the dentist's office getting an X-ray of my teeth. I pretended that my wink would be the magic switch that took the X-ray."

"Did it work?" I asked.

"The producer said that it was the best wink he had ever shot."

I looked at her and wondered if she was going to start talking like a snob again, bragging about her accomplishments. Instead, she did something silly.

Kitty jumped up on the bed and started bouncing. She winked as fast as she could, first one eye and then the other. "Have you ever heard of anything so stupid in your life? They must think I'm three years old. The best wink!" she scoffed. "Dumb, dumb, dumb," she said with each bounce.

I got up on the bed and jumped with her. We reached up and tried to touch the ceiling. I lifted her on a bounce so that she could touch the ceiling.

"Try this," I suggested, jumping high and doing a cheerleading jump in the air.

She tried, but she stuck her tongue out in the middle of the jump. We both ended up rolling around on the bed, laughing out loud.

"Krissy, do you think that I could come to one of the parties that's being filmed?" Kitty asked when we had caught our breaths. "I wouldn't get in the way. I could help. I really could."

"I don't know, Kitty. I'll have to ask the others." I still wasn't sure that I wanted to have her at our parties. I felt self-conscious enough already. But maybe she's right. Maybe she can help. And the Forever Friends Club needs all the help we can get right now!

Eight

WE still had a couple of days to get ready before May Solomon's birthday on Thursday. The teddy bear theme is a popular one. We had already given three parties using teddy bears for the decorations and featuring a teddy bear cake.

Linda Jean liked this theme because she could bring her glass cage filled with teddy bear hamsters to the party. The other two times, she got the parents' permission to give a baby hamster to the birthday child as a special gift. No one can resist those fluffy little balls of fur.

"Luckily, we have all the costumes and decorations from the last teddy bear party. I love the ears and the black nose that you add to your clown costume," Aimee said to me. "I think it's your cutest look."

"Thanks. What kind of craft are you planning this time?" I asked Aimee.

"Since May is only going to be four years old, I thought I'd draw outlines of teddy bears on cardboard, and then have the kids glue colored cotton balls onto the picture. We can trim the edges with yarn for a frame."

It was nice to be sitting around planning a party without worrying about the television show. We had all agreed not to talk or worry about the upcoming event. We were going to get back to the basic idea of Party Time—giving the kids a good time, a fun party that they would always remember as the best party they ever had.

Joy stood up and danced around on the living room sofa. "I need all of you to help me with the dance this time. I thought we'd do "Teddy Bears on Parade." The four of us can form a tunnel with our arms and let the kids go under."

"Do you have the music? We could practice right now," said Linda Jean.

"Of course, I do," said Joy.

Joy pushed the button on her tape player, and sounds of jingling bells mixed with horns and flutes filled the air. "First we act silly and bump into each other like this," Joy instructed, bouncing her hip up against mine.

"Fall down a lot, and run into each other as we try to form the line to have our parade," she directed.

We did as we were told. Every time Aimee and I tried to get into line, we crashed into each other and fell down. We started giggling and almost couldn't hear Joy telling us what to do.

"Okay, march," she said from the front of the line. "Now, form a tunnel by arching your arms up to meet the arms of the person across from you."

We marched, and we formed a laughing, falling, crooked tunnel.

"Then all the kids will keep marching through the tunnel until the music ends. How do you like it?" asked Joy.

"It's easy and fun. The kids will love it," I said.

We all plopped down on the floor, still smiling.

"I'm glad that we're back to normal again," I said. "I have a good feeling about this next party."

"Me, too!"

"Me, three!"

"Me, four!"

Despite my positive attitude and my sister's tips, I was still nervous on Thursday when it was time for May's party.

We arrived two hours early this time, because we had offered to help Mrs. Solomon clean her house before the camera crew arrived. We offered this service free of charge because she was being so nice to let the television people tape May's party.

May is adorable. She is so petite and cute. She has big, brown eyes and long, curly brown hair. She's the type of little girl that you just want to hug. She's helpful, too. She offered to help me set up my magic supplies, and she told me that she wanted to be my personal assistant.

Since we had a little extra time before the party was going to start, I taught her a simple water-glass trick and rehearsed with her as an assistant for part of my act. I put my extra set of teddy bear ears on her head.

The camera crew showed up 30 minutes early. I was glad. This way we had time to tell them where the activities would take place.

They were able to take their positions and be out of the way for the most part.

They took a picture of the cake right away this time.

"I wish I'd had a teddy bear and balloons cake like that when I was a kid," a deep voice said behind me.

Aimee and I turned to meet the eyes of a tall boy with a red WBCC T-shirt.

"Hi, I'm Graham Moore," he introduced himself. "My mom's the producer, but I'm just the gofer," he added. "You must be Aimee," he said, looking at her. "I can tell, because you look just like your dad. You've got the same smile!"

Aimee smiled at that, of course.

"See," he said. "Do you think you'll anchor the evening news one day?"

"Who knows?" she remarked. "Maybe I'll be a famous singer, and you'll produce a documentary on my life."

"Who knows?" he repeated, grinning at her. Then he turned to me.

"You must be Krissy. The clown costume gives you away," he said.

"You seem to know a lot about us," I told him.

"That's a gofer's job. I run errands and memorize people's names so that I can remind the crew and try not to get in the way unless somebody needs me."

"It sounds like a fun job for a high school student," Aimee said.

"Oh, I'm not in high school. I'm going to be in seventh grade next year." I silently congratulated Aimee on her tactics to find out Graham's age.

"I think you have a fan," I whispered a moment later when Graham was called away to run an errand for the crew.

"He is cute, isn't he?" Her eyes followed him around the room where he was unwinding an extension cord.

The doorbell rang. "We'd better get busy with the name tags," I said, dodging the cameras and heading for the door.

May followed along after me. Aimee drew quick teddy bears on each name tag. I wrote the child's name on the tag, and May stuck them on the child. There were only six children at this party. That was a good, manageable number.

I took a deep breath and ignored the TV crew as Kitty had told me to do. I imagined a heavy, black curtain between me and the camera. Even when he zoomed in to get a close shot of May and me, I pretended that it was all happening to some movie star on stage, instead of to me. In fact, I pretended that it was happening to Kitty. That was easy to imagine.

I remembered how cool Kitty had looked sitting on that stage in the Los Angeles studio. She was nervous, but she didn't show it. I tried to be just as cool as she was.

May's parents came in to help with the craft project. That made one older person per child, so the cotton-ball teddies were a breeze.

"Just put a little glue on that edge, May," Aimee said. "What a good job! Now draw the face on it."

"I'm no good at faces," a little girl named Elaine whimpered.

"Just do the best you can," Aimee encouraged.

"I think your bear looks really special," she complimented Mimi, another of May's guests. "Does it have a name?"

"Boo Boo," Mimi declared.

"Is that because he's Yogi Bear's friend?" I asked.

"No, it's because he has a hurt on his knee like I do," she said, showing me her bandage.

"Let's put a bandage on Boo Boo's knee, too," Aimee suggested.

Aimee cut a small square of construction paper and glued it onto the bear's cotton-ball leg. "There, there, Boo Boo. It's all better now."

Mimi smiled and held up her bear to the camera.

When the children were finished making the crafts, Linda Jean showed them her hamsters.

"Oooh, I want one," all the kids said in turn.

"A hamster is a good first pet," Linda Jean said. "When your parents come to pick up all of you, I will give them the information about caring for a hamster. Then they'll have to decide whether or not you can have one."

"If my mommy says that I can have a hamster," Joey asked, "can I have that one?" He pointed to a brown and white ball of fluff in the corner of the cage.

The cameras kept rolling as Linda Jean said, "Let's ask your parents first. But I'll keep that one in mind for you, Joey."

I watched Graham watching Aimee while she sang "Fuzzy Wuzzy" with the kids. He definitely liked her. I could tell.

By the time we got to Joy's dance, the kids were starting to get a little tired. Mimi was leaning on Elaine, and May was complaining about having to put the hamster back into the cage. Everything had gone well so far. I hoped it wasn't going to turn into a crying, screaming mess at that point.

"Who wants to eat cake?" Joy asked.

Those were the magic words.

"Six little voices, plus all the camera people and Graham, shouted, "Me!"

"The only way to get cake is to march in the teddy bear parade," she told them. "May I have some music, please?"

Graham flipped the switch on the tape player.

"We're the silliest bears in the world," Joy told the kids. "We have to line up, but no one knows how to do that. Will you help us?"

The four of us started bumping into each other and falling down. The kids laughed and joined in, trying to push and pull us into a line. Of course, no one knew where the line was supposed to be, so it took about half of the song to get organized. That was the whole idea, naturally.

"Okay, march," Joy said.

We all positioned ourselves between the kids and began our parade around the sofa, behind the table, and over the stool.

"Form the tunnel now!" Joy called.

One by one we guided the kids around in opposite loops to form a tunnel.

"Pass through the teddy bear tunnel, and keep marching to the food table," she instructed.

As if we had rehearsed it a thousand times, the kids marched through the arch that we made with our hands. They went straight to the dining room table and sat down.

Joy and Linda Jean followed the kids to the table, but before we put our hands down, the whole camera crew, the Solomons, and Graham all marched through the tunnel, too, and headed for the cake!

Cake eating and present opening were a snap. We stayed after the party had ended to help with the cleanup, congratulating ourselves repeatedly on our terrific performance.

Graham hung around to help clean up also. Really he stayed to talk to Aimee, but we all pretended not to notice.

"You're a great singer, Aimee," he said.

"You're really talented. Maybe if I do become a producer like my mom, I'll call you to sing on my show."

"That's a long way off, Graham. I have to get through the rest of junior high and high school still. And then there's college, of course."

"You're ambitious, aren't you?" he asked.

"Just like you are!" Aimee replied.

I laughed and looked at Joy. "Graham doesn't know what he's getting into with Aimee," I told her. "She knows boys from every angle after living with all those brothers."

"Yeah, she knows all their sly moves," Joy said. "Graham Moore better watch out."

"So, what's it like having an admirer?" Linda Jean teased Aimee in the car after Abby picked us up. "Did he ask you out on a date?"

"No," Aimee tossed her head. "Who wants to go out on a date? I've got too many boys in my life as it is."

"Brothers don't count, and you know it," I said. "I think you like him more than you're admitting."

"Who has time for boys? I have parties to give, stardom to reach for, pizza pinwheels to roll," Aimee claimed.

"Right, right," Joy scoffed. "We believe every word you say."

We were so busy joking about Graham and Aimee that we forgot all about the party and the filming until Abby asked us how it went.

We stopped laughing and looked at each other. "Well, I guess it went fine," I said. "May is so cute."

"Her friends behaved well," said Linda Jean.

"Everybody liked the cake. You should have seen it, Abby. The TV people all marched through the teddy bear tunnel so that they could eat cake, too. They were more like guests than camera people," Joy told her.

"I had fun. How about you guys?" I asked. Everyone agreed.

"I think you finally got over your fears about being on camera," Abby said. "I'm glad."

"Camera?" I said. "What camera? I didn't notice any camera. Did you?"

"What camera was that?" Joy giggled, socking me playfully in the arm. I leaned over and bumped Aimee.

"There were no cameras at our party," Aimee said, shoving back at me. "There were just teddy bears."

"Yeah, there were fat teddy bears," I said,

pushing back. "But there were no cameras!"

We shoved, pushed, jostled, and giggled until Abby told us to stop.

"I don't care if you tear each other apart," she informed us. "But the car is jumping around all over the road."

Nine

"I wish we didn't have to wait two whole days until the broadcast," I complained to Aimee on the telephone later that night. "Now that it's over with, I can't wait to see the results."

The sound of crunching came over the line. I could tell that Aimee was eating potato chips as she talked. "I know what you mean. I hope they got the tunnel scene on tape. That's bound to be good."

I took a bite of a carrot stick. Anyone else would have thought there was static on the phone line, but we were used to eating and talking at the same time.

"I'm just glad that my nose didn't fall off or that my cards didn't spray out of my hand when I tried to shuffle," I told her. "All in all,

I guess it went pretty well."

"And now we know that we have to plan and stay one step ahead of the kids at all times during a party whether it's for a television show or not."

"I'm sure we could have handled that party at the private school differently. From now on, we should bring extra supplies in case a bunch of extra kids shows up," I suggested.

"Joy was saying that maybe we could actually plan a show with one or two of us on stage at a time while the others roam through the audience, keeping the kids quiet," Aimee remarked. "That way we wouldn't be sending the kids in four different directions at once."

"We also wouldn't have to shout to keep our own groups under control, because everyone would be focused on one thing."

"That's a good idea. I think we should discuss this more with Joy and Linda Jean tomorrow," she said.

We crunched, munched, and talked for awhile longer. Finally, I decided to ask Aimee what she had really thought of Graham Moore.

"I thought he was cute," she admitted, and then she became silent.

"I know. I thought he was cute, too, with

those big brown eyes and that black, curly hair hanging down almost to his eyelashes. I just wondered if you—well—like him?"

"I've only met him one time, Krissy. How am I supposed to know if I like him or not?"

"Well, don't get mad. I was just curious since he's the first boy who has obviously liked one of us. We're not exactly overwhelmed with boyfriends like some of the other girls in junior high are," I said.

Aimee giggled. "Graham's okay, I guess. But I don't have much time for boys. I'm too busy with Party Time."

We left it at that, but I had the feeling that Aimee wasn't telling me the whole truth. I think she was much more interested in Graham Moore than she was admitting to any of us.

We didn't have much time to think about the upcoming broadcast or about boys for the next two days. A last-minute caller asked Abby to cater a meeting of the Atlanta Women's Network, a group of home-based business operators. Abby had just recently become a member.

Their regular caterer canceled at the last minute, and they needed a buffet dinner for

100 people. We spent the next morning and afternoon stuffing baked potatoes with a mixture of stir-fried vegetables and cheese. Abby defrosted several trays of finger foods, and we arranged platters of sliced meats to be heated at the meeting. We didn't have any children to watch, but the Forever Friends Club went to help serve.

There was a speech before the banquet. I thought it would be the usual boring speech, but I was surprised when it was really pretty interesting. Ms. Gloria Reynolds was the speaker, and she talked about success and how to achieve it. She said, "Don't tell me it's impossible until I've already tried it."

I thought that was really impressive. Ms. Reynolds talked about how much her life had improved since she started believing in herself. "Be confident, and have a positive attitude about achieving your goals. Make sure that your goals are ones that you have set, not ones that someone else has set for you."

That really struck a chord with me. I had been spending a lot of time worrying about what other people thought. If I felt down, I blamed Kitty or my parents. Now that I was getting to know Kitty better, it seemed silly to compare myself to her at all. She is her own person, and I am mine.

As for school, so what if I'm smart for my age and younger than anyone else in my grade? I don't have to become separated from my friends just because the school divides us. And I have to do my best because it makes me feel good, not because it pleases my parents or because Mr. Paulo expects a genius.

I was so busy standing there thinking about what Ms. Reynolds said in the beginning of her speech that I didn't even listen to the rest of her speech. I jumped when Joy tapped me on the arm.

"Come on. They're calling us up to the stage," Joy said.

"Why?" I asked.

"I don't know. Let's just go," she directed.

The four of us walked up onto the stage with the speaker. She smiled and shook our hands.

"These young women are an inspiration to us all," she told the group. "They have started their own business and have become successful in a very short amount of time. They have done something that very few entrepreneurs have been able to do. Abby Marshall, our caterer and newest member, tells me that they will even be on WBCC's *Weekend Mag* this Saturday."

Everyone clapped.

We smiled and then started to leave the stage.

"Wait a minute," she called us back. "The Atlanta Women's Network would like to award the four of you with complimentary memberships in our organization." She said our names into the microphone and handed each of us a membership certificate. "Welcome."

She shoved the microphone in front of Linda Jean. "Thank you very much," Linda Jean said without too much hesitation. "We're honored to be a part of your group."

"Is there anything else that you would like to say?" Ms. Reynolds asked, holding the microphone out to the rest of us.

Always ready, Aimee smiled over at me. She took the microphone. "Our fliers are on the table in the lobby. Be sure to pick up one on your way out."

"We could all take a lesson from these young businesswomen," Ms. Reynolds said, as the audience erupted in applause.

"I certainly didn't expect that," Joy said

later as we unloaded the empty trays at her house. "All this attention is kind of exciting, though."

"Exciting?" Linda Jean repeated. "When she shoved that microphone in front of my face and I looked out at all those people, I was so scared I thought I'd be sick!"

That's when I told them about Kitty's tips. I told them about the curtain trick and about pretending that it was someone else in the spotlight and that you were just an observer.

"I guess these tips would work anywhere you had to speak in front of a crowd or be the center of attention. I know they helped me this afternoon at the party," I said.

"I like being the center of attention. I'll bet we're the youngest members of the Atlanta Women's Network," Aimee said.

"Youngest and busiest," I informed them, holding out a list of interested clients.

"I don't think I've ever worked so hard in my life," Joy remarked. She squeezed the leftovers into the refrigerator and plopped down on the rug.

"I guess I should have warned you that people who own their own businesses work practically around the clock," Abby sighed, setting the last carton on the counter. "But I love it!"

We all agreed.

The phone rang as we were nodding our tired heads.

Aimee answered it since the phone was sitting on the table next to her. "Hello, Marshall residence, home of Abby's Catering and Party Time."

She listened for a minute. She covered the mouthpiece with her hand and said, "It's Graham Moore. He says the edited version of the show is ready to preview if we want to see it before it's aired."

We all sat up and nodded our heads more vigorously.

"Tomorrow at one, then," she said. "I'll tell them. He wants what? All right, we'll see you then."

We waited while she listened to Graham. I could swear she was turning red under her dark skin.

"What's he saying?" I whispered.

She signaled me to shush. "Fine," she said. "I'll let you know tomorrow. Good-bye."

"Well?" we all demanded loudly the second she hung up the phone.

"Well, what? Oh, Daddy wants to interview us on camera between showing clips of us working at the parties."

"In the sitting room? The one where he always interviews people on the show?" Joy asked.

"It's no big deal. It's not as wonderful as it looks on television."

After hearing Gloria Reynolds speak, I was up for anything. "Is he going to do it live, or tape it tomorrow when we go to see the preview tape? Should we wear nice clothes or go in grubbies?"

"Graham said he would tape the interview tomorrow so that he can edit it before the show. I'll talk to Daddy about what to wear at home tonight and call everyone in the morning."

"Remember that we have the pool party at three o'clock tomorrow."

"That's no problem. Graham said to come at one o'clock."

"It doesn't matter, anyway. There was a message on the phone machine that the Barkers want to change the pool party to next Wednesday," Abby said.

Then I had another thought. "You know,

Kitty really wanted to come to one of our parties, but I didn't want her to. She's changing. She doesn't seem quite as bratty as she used to be. Plus, not getting that movie role was a real disappointment for her. Would you guys mind if I invited her to the taping tomorrow? I think it would make her feel better."

Aimee looked around. "It's okay with me." Everyone else nodded in agreement.

"So, let's talk more about the interview tomorrow," Aimee said quickly.

"What else did Graham say?" I asked suspiciously. I watched Aimee's face. This time I was sure she was blushing.

Joy, Linda Jean, and Abby all looked at her, too.

"It's nothing to get all worked up about," she said. "He asked me out for a hamburger. That's all."

I shrugged. "You're right. That's no big deal. It's only your first date. That's all!" I exclaimed.

"It's only the first date for the first one of us to be asked out," Joy reminded us. "What did you tell him?"

Aimee grinned. "I said that I didn't have

my calendar with me, and I'd let him know tomorrow," she joked.

We all laughed and threw pillows at her head.

Ten

MY parents drove us to the station. We had decided to wear regular school clothes, instead of either dressing up or wearing our costumes.

Kitty walked beside me as we toured the small news and talk show sets. The WBCC studio wasn't nearly as big as I had expected it to be. Aimee tried to tell us that it was just like a little living room, but it was really only about the size of our kitchen.

"It looks so much bigger on TV," I told her. "I always thought that Mr. Lawrence sat in a real living room, in a real house."

"Look! There's the set for Captain Rick's morning cartoon show," she said, pointing to a small area with the bow of a boat sitting in front.

Captain Rick's boat was a surprise. Instead of a whole boat out on the river, there was only the front part of the boat with a spyglass and a steering wheel and no back of the boat. There was a seating area with a couple of life preservers, a pile of old ropes, and two port holes for effect.

"I wonder if the kids on the show are disappointed that Captain Rick doesn't have a real boat?" Kitty asked.

"It's not nearly as scary this way," I said. "Seeing this makes me wonder what Johnny Carson's set looks like. I mean, does he really have an audience? Or is it all fake, like it is here?"

We walked around a little bit more. Mr. Lawrence let us inspect the camera area and go into the sound booth where they pushed the buttons for sound effects.

"As you can see," he said as we met him back at the *Weekend Mag* set, "there's nothing to be nervous about. You're only talking in front of your parents and the crew, whom you've all met. Graham is here if you need anything, like a drink of water or a tissue. Are you all ready?"

We took our places on the couches next to

Mr. Lawrence's chair. He crossed his legs and told us to get comfortable.

"Let's just practice awhile before we start taping. Just ignore what the camera people are doing. They'll be testing their equipment, getting the lighting right, etc.," Mr. Lawrence told us.

"Here's a typical question that I'll ask you. 'How did you girls get the idea for Party Time?'"

We all just sat there.

"Go ahead. Answer as if this were the real interview," Ms. Moore said from the shadows behind the cameras. "That way you'll know what to say when the show is actually being taped."

Linda Jean spoke first. "It all started when we had a whole summer ahead of us with nothing to do."

Then I spoke up. "We helped take care of the kids at a garden club party, and one of the mothers asked us if we'd like to entertain the kids at her son's birthday party."

"And we would get paid, too," Aimee added. "It sounded like a good idea. We all had our own special talents, so we decided to try it."

"We love our jobs," said Joy. "We get to perform. We all love kids, and it's a great way to spend time with them. Sometimes they do the silliest things. Sometimes they are so sweet. It's great to have a job that you enjoy and get paid for doing, too."

"Yes," Mr. Lawrence admitted. "Many adults wish their jobs were more fulfilling."

I'm not sure when the practicing ended and the show began, but after about 30 minutes of chatting with Mr. Lawrence about everything from what our parties were like when we were kids to what we want to be when we grow up, he held up his hand.

"I think we have enough material here for a documentary, not just a half-hour show. You girls are wonderful on camera. You're all much less nervous than I was my first time on the air," he said.

Ms. Moore came up and shook our hands. "This is going to be fabulous. I'm going to run this video over to the editing department. Will you come back tomorrow and watch the whole show on the big screen as it airs?"

"Sure."

"Of course."

"We wouldn't miss it."

I didn't think I'd be able to wait that long. We didn't have a party to prepare for or food to make for Abby, so we spent the entire next day in the pool. Then we sat around and talked about Graham. Aimee still hadn't told him whether she would go out with him or not.

Finally, it was time to go.

Both Mr. and Mrs. Lawrence were there. I knew Aimee was glad that they left the younger boys at home with Randy. My parents, Kitty, Abby, and Mr. Marshall, who had made a special trip back home from his grocery store route, were there. Mr. Jacobs, Linda Jean's dad, was there, too. Ms. Moore and Graham joined us in the big viewing room.

Graham turned on the TV and came over to sit by Aimee.

Suddenly, we saw the picture of us sitting around Mr. Lawrence on the television set. Then the picture narrowed to just him. He said, "Tonight I'd like to introduce Atlanta's newest and youngest business team. And this is a special treat for me, because one of these talented young women is my own daughter, Aimee."

"I don't remember him saying that," Aimee whispered.

Graham leaned over to tell her, "He taped his introduction after you all left yesterday.

They mix everything together in the editing room so that it looks like the show is all done at one time. It's amazing, isn't it?"

"It sure is," Aimee agreed.

"Oh, look! There's Linda Jean telling how we got started," I said, calling attention to the screen. "Hey, that's when you said we were just practicing!"

"Whatever works," Mr. Lawrence joked.

"That was sneaky, Daddy, really sneaky," Aimee said.

"Oh, I look awful!" Joy wailed. "And I look fat. I missed a step in the tunnel dance. Do you think anyone noticed?"

"That's the shadow of the potted plant," I told her. "Calm down. You look great. It's me who looks like a blimp in my clown suit. Do I really jump around that much?" I asked.

"Yes," Linda Jean said. "But the kids love it. At least people can't tell who you are in that outfit. I didn't realize Mimi was squeezing that guinea pig at the party. I wondered why the poor thing was so quiet when we got home. I'll never make zookeeper of the year this way."

Aimee was watching herself sing on the set. "Hey, I'm pretty good," she admitted. "I don't know what your problems are, you guys. I think I look fine on TV."

"And modesty is one of your strong points," I teased.

"Well, I think she looks good, too," Graham added. "It must run in the family."

"Oh, brother!" I rolled my eyes and watched the credits roll across the screen.

"So, what'd you think?" Ms. Moore asked, beaming.

"It was great!" exclaimed Joy.

"It was okay, I guess," ventured Linda Jean.

"It was different than I had expected it to be," I said.

"Oh, come on, you guys. It was great! I loved it!" Aimee cried.

We all smiled then and started talking at once. We went over the good points, the rough spots, and the so-so areas. Ms. Moore took us all out to dinner, and we continued to talk about the show between bites.

Then the most amazing thing happened. A couple approached our table and introduced themselves as the Browns.

"Are you the girls we saw on *Weekend Mag* tonight?"

We all nodded.

"What a wonderful idea," Mrs. Brown said. "We've been looking for a service like yours since we moved to town six months ago. Do you have business cards? We'd like to call you for our next party."

Aimee handed her a flier.

"Will you sign it?" Mr. Brown asked. "You're celebrities now, so we need your autographs for our collection."

We giggled and passed the flier around the table for everyone to sign it.

"I can't believe it," Aimee said. "Someone actually wanted my autograph."

More people came up to the table to say that they had seen the show and to ask us for fliers.

Aimee was really in her element. I could almost see the stars in her eyes. I knew that she was pretty far gone when she asked Kitty for advice about modeling and doing comercials.

"I'd be happy to give you a few tips," Kitty said, smiling at me.

"That's great! Why don't you come over to Joy's house on Monday after your dance class?"

I looked at Aimee in amazement. "You're

asking my sister over for a visit?" I hissed. "She's nine years old, for gosh sakes. I can tell you everything she told me."

"Forget it, Kitty. You got to come yesterday and today. Don't push your luck," I told her.

Kitty ignored my warning. "I'll be there at three o'clock if it's okay with Mom and Dad. Maybe I could come over every day and help out all of you with Party Time. I can dance and sing and—"

"Mother!" I insisted.

Mom cleared her throat. "Kitty, dear, I don't think you're old enough to help out with Party Time."

"But, Mom!" Kitty cried.

"No, Krissy is right. Maybe when you are older, you can start a business of your own. Then you can ask your sister for advice."

She might have protested more if some-one hadn't come up to the table just then and asked for *her* autograph.

I heaved a sigh of relief. It was a small victory, but a victory, anyway.

For awhile, we ate our pizza in silence. Fame makes you very hungry. Between his third and fourth piece I heard Graham ask Aimee out again. She finally said *yes.*

That was one less thing I had to worry about, I thought.

The cheese from my piece of pizza stretched out from my mouth, and I quickly lifted it into my mouth. I thought about all the disasters over the last two weeks. Now things were going well again, and I had made some resolutions that I hoped would make my life easier.

"What do you think the Forever Friends Club should try next?" Aimee leaned close to ask.

I smiled at the group. Everyone was talking about the show and about our plans for the future. We even joked about starting a Forever Friends Fan Club.

"The sky's the limit!" I shouted. "Together, we can do anything!"

About the Author

CINDY SAVAGE lives in a big rambling house on a tiny farm in northern California with her husband, Greg, and her four children, Linda, Laura, Brian, and Kevin.

She published her first poem in a local newspaper when she was six years old, and soon after got hooked on reading and writing. After college she taught bilingual Spanish/English preschool, then took a break to have her own children. Now she stays home with her kids and writes magazine articles and books for children and young adults.

In her spare time, she plays with her family, reads, does needlework, bakes bread, and tends the garden.

Traveling has always been one of her favorite hobbies. As a child she crossed the United States many times with her parents, visiting Canada and Mexico along the way. Now she takes shorter trips to the ocean and the mountains to get recharged. She gets her inspiration to write from the places she visits and the people she meets along the way.